A Children's Book of Short Stories

The 3 W Boys

By Raebeth Costolo

tate publishing
CHILDREN'S DIVISION

Published by Tate Publishing & Enterprises, LLC
127 E. Trade Center Terrace | Mustang, Oklahoma 73064 USA
1.888.361.9473 | www.tatepublishing.com

Tate Publishing is committed to excellence in the publishing industry. The company reflects the philosophy established by the founders, based on Psalm 68:11,
"The Lord gave the word and great was the company of those who published it."

Book design copyright © 2014 by Tate Publishing, LLC. All rights reserved.
Cover and interior design by Errol Villamante
Illustrations by Lucent Ouano

Published in the United States of America

ISBN: 978-1-63367-345-8
Juvenile Fiction / Boys & Men
14.09.25

To all my family who have given me many blessings. To the men in my life: my husband, my son, my grandson, and my father.

In Memory Of

child family friend

Michael Malone

Brothers Stick Together

Wellington, Weston, and Wallace Williams were brothers who lived at 225 Baker Street, Evergreen, Colorado. Wellington was 10, Weston was 7, and Wallace was 5. The boys loved being in Colorado because there were so many fun things to do: You could go snow skiing on the mountains; you could build a big snowman because there was always lots of snow in the winter; you could fish in the beautiful streams during the summer; and you could camp in the mountains with wonderful scenery right at your doorstep.

Wellington watched over his two younger brothers because he was the oldest. Their mother always said, *"You boys stick together because that's what brothers do."* The boys liked playing together.

Summer had come, and the boys decided they wanted to go fishing at the stream not far from their house. Their mother said, "Let's have fish for dinner tonight." The boys gathered up their fishing poles and headed for the stream. On the way, they stopped at the bait shop to get worms for their fishing hooks. Arriving at the stream, each was boasting how many fish he was going to catch and take home to their mother!

But no sooner had they arrived, when little Wallace slipped on a rock and fell into the stream! *The current was beginning to carry him away!* But Wellington thought quickly and threw a rope from his back pack to his younger brother. Wallace caught it, and Wellington pulled him over to safety. They did not catch any fish.

Wellington decided it was best to go home since Wallace was soaking wet. When they started to tell their mother what happened, all three boys were disappointed they did not have any fish for dinner. But their mother understood and was so glad that Wallace was safe. "I am very proud of all you boys," she said. *"You remembered that brothers stick together."*

The 3 W Boys Visit
Grandma and Grandpa

School was out for the year, and Wellington, Weston, and Wallace Williams were excited to begin their summer vacation in Colorado. Besides all the fun things they got to do during the summer like fishing, biking, and camping, this year their family was going to visit Grandma and Grandpa in Glenwood Springs. They couldn't wait! Today was the day they were going!

It was always fun to visit Grandma and Grandpa. Grandma would let the boys help her cook in the kitchen. Grandpa would let the boys help him in his garden. Grandpa's favorite hobby was growing his own flowers to decorate all the flowerbeds at their home.

The drive to Glenwood Springs took two hours by car. The boys kept busy playing games on the electronic tablet their father let them borrow. Grandma and Grandpa were so happy to see the family! Grandpa was ready for all his grandsons to help him. He had the flower seedlings ready to be put into the flowerbeds. Wellington, Weston, and Wallace worked all afternoon planting with Grandpa.

Later, Grandma had the boys wash the dirt off their hands so they could help her bake cookies. But Grandma had a little surprise for the boys. She had sewn them each special baking aprons! Wellington's had Transformers on it. Weston's had Spiderman on it. Wallace's had Batman on it. Each took turns in the steps of preparing the cookie dough. Wellington put the flour in the bowl; Weston put the sugar in the bowl; and Wallace added the chocolate chips! Soon, Grandma was spooning the dough on the cookie sheets for baking. The cookies smelled so good as they baked! Grandma promised to serve the cookies later as a bedtime snack.

After dinner the boys took baths. They were thinking about the cookies. Grandma poured milk in glasses and served the cookies they had helped to bake. Yum! They tasted good! Later, Grandpa read a bed-time story to all of them. Then, Grandma kissed each of them good-night. As the boys settled into their beds, the same thought kept going through their minds, *"There is no place like home--except Grandma's and Grandpa's."*

Wellington Williams Helps a Friend

Wellington Williams was lucky. He was smart and did well in school. When his teacher asked for volunteers to help her, Wellington always volunteered to help others with their lessons. He liked being with his friends either at school or in his neighborhood.

His mother, Mrs. Williams, also helped as Room Mother at the boys' school. Sometimes she helped bake cupcakes for special occasions. Sometimes she would volunteer to help the teacher with a class craft project. All the children knew Mrs. Williams and always said, "Hi, Mrs. Williams!" She liked seeing all the other children on her visits. Some of the children would run up to Mrs. Williams and give her a big hug!

As Christmas was approaching, Wellington's class was planning a Christmas party. Wellington's teacher asked Mrs. Williams if she could help at the party. The children were getting excited about the holidays! Mrs. Williams was glad to lend a hand.

When the day of the party arrived, Mrs. Williams walked into Wellington's classroom and could not find Wellington! She looked around the room carefully, but she did not see him. She asked Jimmy Snow if he knew where Wellington was. Jimmy quickly replied, "Oh, yes, Mrs. Williams. Wellington volunteered to help Jason Smith with his math lesson, but they needed to use the computer in the library. Wellington told the teacher he did not mind missing some of the party." Mrs. Williams was proud of her son.

That night as Wellington was getting ready for bed, his mother told him she was proud he had helped Jason Smith with his math. She said she did not think many children would want to miss part of a class party. Wellington replied, *That's what friends are for.*

Wellington, Weston, and Wallace Bake Bread

Mr. Williams had a wonderful hobby. He liked to bake bread from scratch! Mr. Williams began baking bread when Wellington was a baby. By now, he was very good at it! He could make white bread, cinnamon swirl bread, and yummy pecan sticky buns, which were three inches thick and oozing with delicious sauce!

He told each of the boys they could help him whenever they wanted, but he reminded them that baking bread from scratch took five hours from start to finish. Mr. Williams told the boys you had to wait several minutes between baking steps so this would take patience.

Today, it was snowing outside, and it was very cold. Mr. Williams thought this would be a perfect day for baking bread. All three boys wanted to help. Wellington measured the flour and other ingredients in preparation for creating the bread dough. Later, after the dough had risen enough times, Weston helped knead the dough. Mr. Williams showed him how to push and roll the dough. Wallace liked to help form the dough into long loaves ready to go into the pans. As the bread was baking, it smelled so good in the kitchen!

When their mother called the boys to dinner that evening, the boys were anxious to try the bread they helped to make. It tasted delicious!

As Mrs. Williams was cleaning the kitchen and putting things away that evening, she came across the bread recipe card. Flour was all over the card! She smiled. She realized it did not matter. What mattered was the three boys had shared an afternoon together with their father. She thought to herself, *"Maybe some day the boys will teach their children how to make home-made bread."*

Weston Plays Soccer

Weston Williams liked to play soccer! He played on two soccer teams. Many of his friends also played on both soccer teams. Weston liked to wear his special red sweat band when playing soccer. Weston liked to score. But his Dad told him it was important to also pass the soccer ball to a teammate during the games. Weston's coach made sure that each boy on the team got a turn playing. Sometimes a boy needed to rest on the sidelines in order to give everyone on the team a chance to play.

Today their team was playing another team known for winning. Some of the boys on the opposing team were older. Weston was determined his team could win. As they began playing, his friend, Jason Ryan, kicked the ball right to Weston. Weston carefully moved his feet to get the ball down to the net. He moved again. Score! Halftime came. Everyone playing got to have a drink of cold water.

The game began again, and this time Weston's friend, Jason, had the ball. It looked like Jason would score, but just as he got down to the net, he kicked the ball over to Weston, and Weston was ready. He kicked the ball into the net! He had scored two goals! They won!

That night as Weston was getting ready to go to bed, Mrs. Williams told him how proud she was that he scored the goals. He was happy also. But Weston realized *sometimes you get to win things by yourself, and sometimes it takes others on your team to help*.

Wallace Turns Into a Raccoon

It was late October, and the leaves were nearly gone off the beautiful golden Aspen trees in the Rocky Mountains. Halloween was around the corner, and the three Williams boys could not wait to go trick-or-treating with their friends.

Wallace liked art class at school. Wallace was good at art. Today his teacher was handing out very different art supplies to the children. She gave each child a pair of plastic gloves. She announced they would be making soft plaster masks for Halloween. She told the children to decide what they wanted to make. Wallace thought for a moment. Then he got his idea: He decided to make a raccoon face!

It was a good thing the children had plastic gloves. The mixture to make the masks was very sticky and messy. The children finished their masks and placed them on a rack to dry. A few days passed, and the masks had dried. It was time to paint the masks. Wallace carefully filled in stripes and whiskers on the mask. It turned out just like a raccoon!

After school, Wallace said to his mother, "Mom, I need you to make me a raccoon suit for Halloween because I made a mask in my art class." Even though Mrs. Williams was good at sewing, she never had sewn a raccoon suit. She went to the store and got two colors of fuzzy material which looked like fur. She knew she would need to make a striped tail made of the two different colors—just like a real raccoon. That evening, Mrs. Williams began working on the costume. It was going to take more time than she thought to complete.

In the morning after the boys went to school, Mrs. Williams finished the costume. It was perfect! It was a good thing the costume was warm and cozy. The afternoon of Halloween it began lightly snowing! That evening when the boys went trick-or-treating, Wallace was nice and warm being a raccoon—*thanks to Mom!*

# e|LIVE

listen|imagine|view|experience

AUDIO BOOK DOWNLOAD INCLUDED WITH THIS BOOK!

In your hands you hold a complete digital entertainment package. In addition to the paper version, you receive a free download of the audio version of this book. Simply use the code listed below when visiting our website. Once downloaded to your computer, you can listen to the book through your computer's speakers, burn it to an audio CD or save the file to your portable music device (such as Apple's popular iPod) and listen on the go!

How to get your free audio book digital download:

1. Visit www.tatepublishing.com and click on the e|LIVE logo on the home page.
2. Enter the following coupon code:
   83bd-bd1b-9c95-8c3b-daf8-7753-94a1-5c87
3. Download the audio book from your e|LIVE digital locker and begin enjoying your new digital entertainment package today!